LEADERS OF THE SCIENTIFIC REVOLUTION™

ROBERT BOYLE

Alexis Burling

Rosen YA
New York

Published in 2018 by The Rosen Publishing Group, Inc.
29 East 21st Street, New York, NY 10010

Copyright © 2018 by The Rosen Publishing Group, Inc.

First Edition

All rights reserved. No part of this book may be reproduced in any form without permission in writing from the publisher, except by a reviewer.

Library of Congress Cataloging-in-Publication Data

Names: Burling, Alexis.
Title: Robert Boyle / Alexis Burling.
Description: New York, NY : Rosen Publishing, 2018. | Series: Leaders of the scientific revolution | Audience: Grades 7–12. | Includes bibliographical references and index.
Identifiers: LCCN 2016055890 | ISBN 9781508174769 (library bound book)
Subjects: LCSH: Boyle, Robert, 1627–1691. | Chemists—Great Britain—Biography—Juvenile literature. | Scientists—Great Britain—Biography—Juvenile literature. | Chemistry—History—17th century—Juvenile literature. | Great Britain—History—Stuarts, 1603–1714—Juvenile literature.
Classification: LCC Q143.B77 B87 2018 | DDC 509.2 [B] —dc23
LC record available at https://lccn.loc.gov/2016055890

Manufactured in China

CONTENTS

INTRODUCTION 4

CHAPTER ONE
THE EARLY YEARS: THE BIRTH OF A
SCIENTIFIC MIND 9

CHAPTER TWO
SOLITUDE AND STUDY 24

CHAPTER THREE
BOYLE'S BREAKTHROUGHS 37

CHAPTER FOUR
THE FATHER OF CHEMISTRY 53

CHAPTER FIVE
FROM SCIENCE TO SALVATION:
THE LONDON CHAPTER 68

CHAPTER SIX
BOYLE'S LEGACY 80

TIMELINE 95
GLOSSARY 97
FOR MORE INFORMATION 99
FOR FURTHER READING 103
BIBLIOGRAPHY 105
INDEX 108

INTRODUCTION

During much of the period known as the Middle Ages (approximately 500–1500 CE), science was a relatively static field. Influenced by the religious teachings of the Catholic Church, as well as scientific and mathematical theories developed by ancient Greeks such as Aristotle, Euclid, and Ptolemy, most Europeans accepted a core set of ideas as truth. Earth is the center of the universe. Planets and the Sun revolve around Earth in circular orbits. The velocity of an object is directly proportional to the amount of force acting on it.

But beginning in the mid-1500s, scientific thinking began to shift. In an era that stretched to the early eighteenth century and was later called the Scientific Revolution, a number of instrumental scholars made powerful discoveries that changed the way society regarded the natural world. Just before his death in 1543, Nicolaus Copernicus published *De Revolutionibus Orbium Coelestium* (*On the Revolutions of the Heavenly Spheres*). This groundbreaking work challenged commonly held beliefs and biblical scripture by describing a heliocentric model of the solar system. It suggested that Earth and other planets revolve around the Sun.

Nicolaus Copernicus maintained that the Sun was the center of the universe. A statue of the influential man still sits near the castle where he lived in Olsztyn, Poland.

Johannes Kepler and Galileo Galilei built on Copernicus's ideas. In 1609, Kepler developed the first of three laws of planetary motion, which stated that the planets' paths around the Sun are elliptical, not circular. Around the same time period, Galileo overturned Aristotle's laws of motion. He proved that a body moving at a constant speed does not need to be pushed by a force to continue moving. In addition, the speed of a freely falling object does not depend on its mass, as Aristotle had claimed. These theories were controversial at the time. Galileo was convicted of heresy for supporting Copernicus's heliocentric view of the universe and spent years under house arrest. Still, his findings had long-lasting consequences that shaped the future of science in Europe and across the globe.

One of the most significant people in the Scientific Revolution was Robert Boyle. Born in Ireland in 1627, he is often referred to as the father of chemistry. He was the mastermind behind Boyle's law, which explains the inverse relationship between the pressure and volume of a gas—in basic terms, gases respond to pressure changes by increasing or decreasing their volume. In 1660, Boyle helped found the Royal Society in London, a group dedicated to supporting and advancing scientific study throughout the world that exists to this day. He also published dozens of books, articles, and scholarly papers over the course of his lifetime, including *New*

Introduction

on^{ble} Robert Boyle.

Though not as well known today as Copernicus, Robert Boyle made groundbreaking discoveries in chemistry and physics and published more than thirty works during his lifetime.

Experiments Physico-Mechanicall, Touching the Spring of the Air and Its Effects (1660), *The Sceptical Chymist* (1661), and *Excellency of Theology, Compar'd with Natural Philosophy* (1674).

Today, Boyle's name isn't as recognizable as those of Galileo or Isaac Newton. Boyle lived a solitary existence for long stretches and spent a lot of his free time in a laboratory. But without his innovative contributions, the Scientific Revolution would have been incomplete. "Unquestionably, Boyle was one of the key figures in the 'scientific revolution' of the seventeenth century," wrote Michael Hunter in his biography of Boyle. "[He] played a central role in the reformulation of knowledge about the natural world and man's place in it which occurred at that time and which has formed the basis of scientific developments ever since."

CHAPTER ONE

The Early Years: The Birth of a Scientific Mind

On January 25, 1627, Robert Boyle was born in County Waterford, Ireland—a country that, at the time, was under the control of England. He was the fourteenth child, with six brothers and eight sisters. His parents—the English-born Richard Boyle, first Earl of Cork, and Richard's second wife, Lady Catherine Fenton, who was the daughter of Ireland's secretary of state—were extraordinarily wealthy. They split their time between a lavish medieval estate called Lismore Castle and various other properties on 42,000 acres (17,000 ha) scattered throughout Ireland.

For most of his childhood, Robert was raised in a Protestant household and was surrounded by luxury. Lismore Castle, where he spent the majority of his time, overlooked the Blackwater River. It had a gatehouse,

Constructed in 1185, Lismore Castle was sold to Richard Boyle by Sir Walter Raleigh in 1602. Richard's son Robert was born here in 1627.

riding stables, and a chapel in addition to its main quarters. A beautiful garden with regal hedges, elaborate walls, and flowers constantly in bloom completed the sprawling manor. Inside, the rooms were filled with expensive wall tapestries, flowing drapes, and ornate furniture.

Robert's mother died suddenly in childbirth when Robert was three years old. From then on, because their father traveled often, Robert and his siblings were looked after by a rotating army of servants. There were cooks, porters, grooms, and footmen who managed the

The Early Years: The Birth of a Scientific Mind

daily affairs of the household. Construction workers and gardeners kept the castle's appearance in immaculate shape. Musicians, nurses, and private tutors occupied the children, teaching them lessons in Latin, Greek, and French. As Robert wrote in his autobiography, *An Account of Philaretus During His Minority*, he was raised "in a condition that neither was high enough to prove a temptation to laziness, nor low enough to discourage [me] from aspiring." In the same memoir, he expressed relief at being one of the younger (instead of elder) sons of a powerful family, because,

> **to a person, whose humour indisposes him to the distracting hurry of the world, the being born heir to a great family is but a glittering kind of slavery, whilst obliging him to a public entangled course of life, to support the credit of his family, and tying him from satisfying his dearest inclinations, it often forces him to build the advantages of his house upon the ruins of his own contentment.**

From the moment Robert was born, he basked in his privileged lifestyle. But he was also often ill. He suffered from a debilitating speech impediment—he developed a stutter before he turned ten. Despite doctors' attempts to fix the problem, Robert's stammer continued for the rest of his life.

RICHARD BOYLE, A COMPLEX FIGURE

Born on October 13, 1566, in Canterbury, England, Richard Boyle lived a gilded but complicated life. Over the course of his career, he became one of the richest and most influential men in Ireland. He was appointed the first Earl of Cork in 1620, Lord High Justice in 1629, and Lord High Treasurer in 1631.

But with power often comes corruption. In some instances, Richard obtained and managed his land in suspect ways. He was imprisoned for two years in England for embezzlement in 1598. Years later, a number of his estates had defective titles, and he was fined heavily for these mistakes in 1633. By the time of his death in 1643, he had lost much of his political pull in the region.

AN ELITE EDUCATION

Because Richard was hardly home to attend to his children, many of them were sent away to be educated at exclusive schools elsewhere. On October 2, 1635, when Robert was eight years old, he and his twelve-year-old brother, Francis, set sail for Windsor, England, across

The Early Years: The Birth of a Scientific Mind

the Irish Sea. They had been accepted to Eton College, a prestigious boarding school for boys from aristocratic families. When they arrived, they were taken under the wing of Sir Henry Wotton, a senior administrator at the school and a long-time friend of their father's.

Today, Eton College is a prestigious boarding school for teen boys that offers a full range of classes, from science and math to music and drama. But in

Eton College was founded in 1440 by King Henry VI. At that time, most of the boys who attended went on to King's College in Cambridge to further their education.

Robert Boyle's day, life at Eton was very different—and strict. Boys slept two or three to a bed and were at their desks by 6 a.m. every morning. Lessons finished at 8 p.m. All classes were taught in Latin, the language of the church.

When not in class, the boys' behavior and activities were extremely regimented and monitored closely. They walked in two straight lines to every class and never yelled or were rowdy. If they weren't speaking Latin or wore rumpled clothing, the boys got in trouble and were made to serve detention. Two meals were served a day—except on Friday, which was reserved for a day of fasting.

Eton boys went to class for most of the year and rarely saw their families. They were allowed two holidays, each three weeks in duration. One took place at Christmas, though the boys were not permitted to return home. The other holiday was in the summer. It was a long school year, and many boys got homesick. But most parents felt the education and the enforcement of discipline was well worth it.

Robert spent more than three years at Eton. He got up at 5:30 every morning and went to church. He then attended a variety of classes, including music, drama, French, and Latin. Two hours out of each day were dedicated to writing. During his spare free time, Robert read historical accounts and romances.

Drawn by G. Clint A.R.A. Engraved by E. Engleheart.

SIR HENRY WOTTON.

Sir Henry Wotton was the provost of Eton College during Robert Boyle's tenure at the school. He was also a renowned poet and served in Parliament in 1614 and 1625.

According to letters Sir Wotton wrote to the boys' father during the school year, both Robert and his brother were "very studious and diligent ... highly respected and very well beloved." Over time, however, Francis performed less well than his brother. Soon, Richard became disillusioned with his sons' experiences at Eton. In a letter to a friend, Richard wrote, "I vowe onto you they were better schollers when they came out of Ireland then they are now which greevs my very soule."

At the end of 1638, Richard pulled Robert and Francis out of Eton permanently. He sent the boys to Stalbridge Manor, one of his properties in Dorset, England. For a brief few months, the brothers continued their studies under Isaac Marcombes, a private tutor. Fifteen-year-old Francis was married off to Elizabeth Killigrew, an Englishwoman from an equally aristocratic family. But the nuptials didn't deter Richard from furthering his sons' education. Four days after the wedding, Robert and Francis were once again sent abroad in the name of learning—this time, to Europe.

THE GRAND TOUR

In the autumn of 1639—when Robert was twelve—he, Francis, Isaac Marcombes, and two servants embarked on a grand adventure. Their first stop: France. From the capital city of Paris, they continued on to Moulins,

GENEUE. Genff.

Robert's time in Geneva was a fruitful one. The city's scenic Alps and close proximity to Lake Geneva gave the young boy plenty of time to contemplate God and nature.

Lyons, and Geneva, Switzerland, where they spent nearly two years at Marcombes's childhood home. There, Robert learned logic, mathematics, rhetoric, geography, and religious instruction. On off hours, he rode horses and was schooled in dancing, fencing, and tennis.

While in Geneva, Robert prayed daily and attended church twice a week. But it wasn't until a mysterious thunderstorm that he found his true connection to God. According to his autobiography, Robert was awakened one summer night by booming thunder and shards of lightning cutting across the sky. The noise from the wind was so loud and the storm so violent that he thought he was in serious danger. He made a promise to himself that if he survived the night, he would be "more Religiously [and] watchfully employ'd." This event, which took place in December 1640, marked the beginning of what became for Robert a life-long devotion to Christian beliefs and devout religious study.

Nearly a year later, in September 1641, Robert, Francis, and Marcombes journeyed to Italy for an extended stay. After making their way through Venice and other northern cities, they arrived in Florence toward the end of October. Later, they traveled to Rome and saw the pope. In these bustling cities filled with art, scrumptious food, and melodious music, they immersed themselves in the country's culture. They spoke Italian and read volumes about Italy's history. Marcombes also took the boys to various brothels, though Robert insists in his autobiography that he never had sex nor did anything disreputable.

It was during this time in Italy that Robert heard about the teachings of Galileo. The esteemed scientist—to whom Boyle referred in *An Account of Philaretus During His Minority* as "the great star-gazer Galileo"—was living outside Florence and continued to do so until his death on January 8, 1642. Though Robert never met Galileo in person, this early introduction to the man's teachings about gravity, motion, and the workings of

The Early Years: The Birth of a Scientific Mind

GALILEO'S IMPACT

Galileo Galilei was born on February 15, 1564, in Pisa, Italy. Throughout the course of his life as a mathematics and astronomy teacher, Galileo made many important contributions to science. After building a telescope, he found that Earth's moon was not flat but curved and filled with craters. He was also the first to discover four of Jupiter's revolving moons and that Venus has phases, much like Earth's moon does.

In 1612, Galileo published a book called *Discorso intorno alle cose, che stanno in sù l'acqua, ò che in quella si muovono* (generally known as the *Discourse on Bodies in Water*). In it, he rejected Aristotle's explanation of why objects float in water. Unlike Aristotle, who believed it was because of their flat shape, Galileo argued that the relationship between how much an object weighed was directly proportional to how much water was displaced. The heavier the object, the more water it displaces.

Perhaps Galileo's most famous discovery happened early in his career when he was the head of mathematics at the University of Pisa. Though scholars have conflicting opinions about what actually took place, the story goes that in 1589, Galileo

(CONTINUED ON THE NEXT PAGE)

Robert Boyle

(CONTINUED FROM THE PREVIOUS PAGE)

climbed to the top of the Leaning Tower of Pisa. From there he dropped two objects, each weighing a different amount. The objects reached the ground at different times. But it wasn't because one was heavier than the other. Instead, it was because each object was affected by air friction differently. If this experiment were replicated in a vacuum, these same two objects would reach the ground simultaneously. This disproved Aristotle's theory that the speed of a falling object was proportional to its weight.

Galileo altered the course of scientific history by proposing that bodies in free fall drop at a uniform speed determined by gravity, not by their weight.

THE EARLY YEARS: THE BIRTH OF A SCIENTIFIC MIND

the universe had a profound impact on the rest of his life. It fueled Robert's growing interest in mysticism and scientific study.

BAD NEWS ON THE HORIZON

By 1642, Richard Boyle's finances had become considerably strained. While Robert and Francis were flitting back and forth across Europe, a civil war had broken out at home. Sparked by the Irish Rebellion of 1641, when a small group of landowners attempted to take over Dublin Castle and demanded equal rights for Catholics, a bloody eleven-year struggle for power had erupted between the Catholics and Protestants in Ireland. The Royalists, loyal to King Charles I, and Parliamentarians became embroiled in their own nine-year skirmish over who would retain control of the government in England.

Sensing trouble, Richard requested an end to his sons' travels. Consequently, 19-year-old Francis joined the army and got involved with the fighting in Ireland. Just 15 at the time, Robert refused. Instead, he returned with Marcombes to Geneva, where he remained involved in his studies for another two years.

Robert's whirlwind tour of Europe did wonders for his education, both in school and socially. But it came at a steep cost. His brother Lewis, whom Robert hadn't seen since before his departure to Europe, was killed in

Robert Boyle

During the Irish Rebellion of 1641, Irish Catholics attempted to overthrow the Protestant regime. Though historians' records differ, an estimated 12,000 Protestants were killed during the conflict.

The Early Years: The Birth of a Scientific Mind

the Battle of Liscarroll. Then on September 15, 1643, Richard Boyle became ill and died. With little money left for his studies without his father's support, Robert returned to England in the summer of 1644. He was 17, and his journey to become one of the Scientific Revolution's greatest thinkers was just getting started.

CHAPTER TWO

Solitude and Study

By 1644, the English Civil Wars, often referred to as the Great Rebellion, had been raging for two years. Based in Oxford, King Charles I controlled the north and west of England, Wales, and most of Ireland. In contrast, Parliament had jurisdiction over southern and eastern England, London (England's financial capital), and many of the territory's key trading ports. The king's army needed London in order to secure a definitive lead in the fighting. But on July 2, the Parliamentarians eked out a major win over the Royalists in the Battle of Marston Moor. It was a victory that caused a shift in the balance of power that would eventually lead to a Royalist defeat in the years to come.

When the thin and sunburned 17-year-old Robert Boyle returned to England that summer, he found

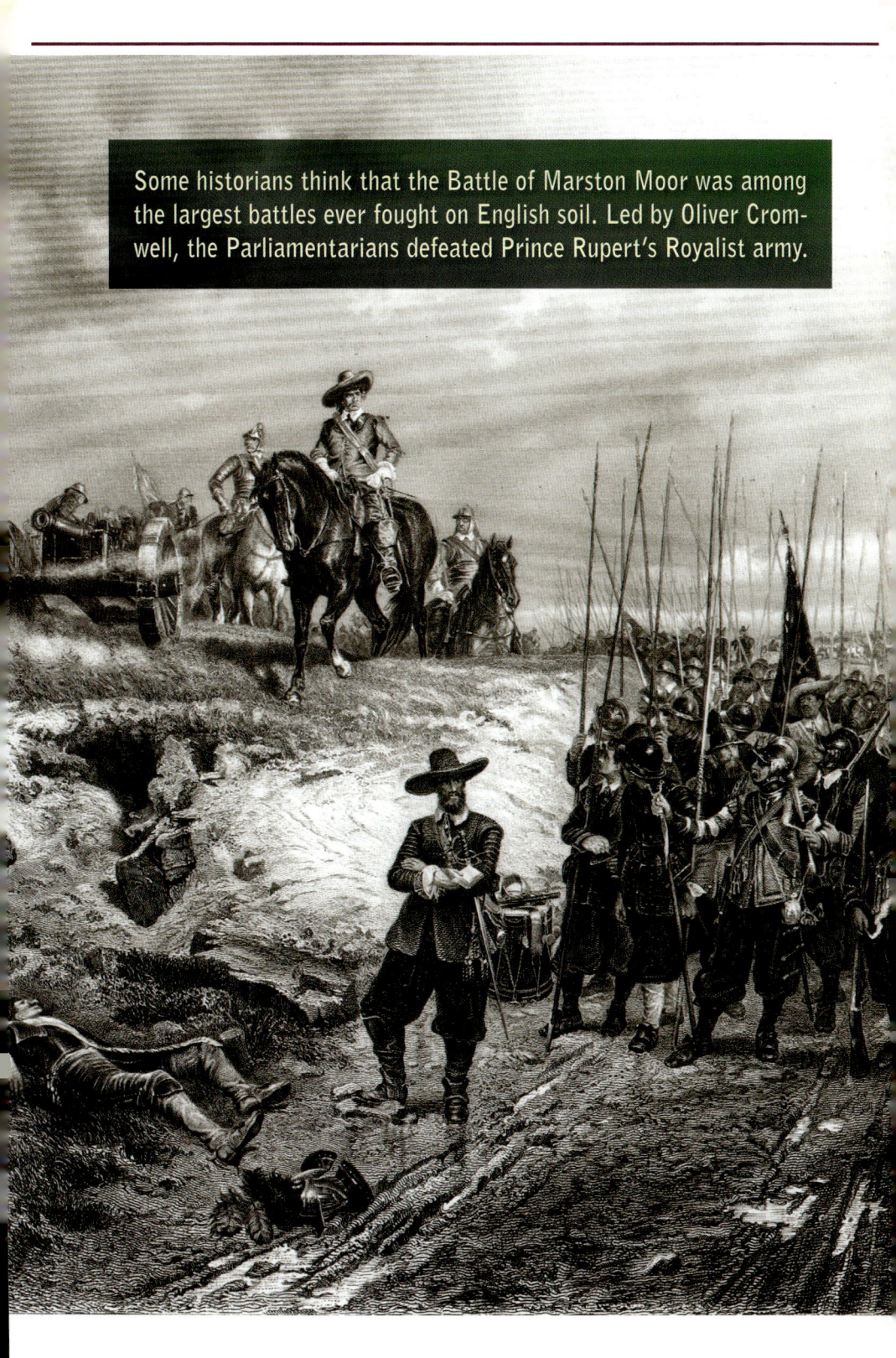

Some historians think that the Battle of Marston Moor was among the largest battles ever fought on English soil. Led by Oliver Cromwell, the Parliamentarians defeated Prince Rupert's Royalist army.

the world he used to inhabit during his Eton College days to be a strange and divided place. But rather than enlist in combat like his brothers did, he stayed neutral and, instead, focused on furthering his studies. Though his father had left him estates in England and Ireland as part of his inheritance, Boyle was relatively broke after five years of traveling abroad. For roughly four months, he lived with his 30-year-old sister Katherine in London to regain his footing.

    Boyle's first short stint in London after coming home was both eye-opening and invigorating. For all hours of the day, he was surrounded by Katherine's close social acquaintances. Unlike their father's Royalist connections, Katherine's friends were Parliamentarians. Robert learned a great deal about their political vision for the future and their critiques of the Royalist cause. When it came time for Robert to depart and claim his rightful ownership of Stalbridge, it was a Parliamentarian escort who made sure he remained safe along his journey to Dorset.

LADY RANELAGH

Robert Boyle was one of the greatest scientists of the seventeenth century. It could be argued that he couldn't have accomplished so much if it weren't for his sister Katherine, Lady Ranelagh. But Katherine wasn't only Robert's patron. She had some smarts of her own.

At the time, women were considered the inferior sex. Men like Richard Boyle, Katherine's father, thought girls should be bred only to attract wealthy marriage prospects. She was sent to live with a potential husband's family when she was not even ten years old. In 1630, when she was just 15, she was married off to Arthur Jones, heir to Viscount Ranelagh. The union was an unhappy one—the couple basically lived separate lives.

But despite her unfortunate relationship, Katherine made the best of it. She made friends with prominent thinkers and philosophers of the day, including Robert's colleague Samuel Hartlib. Always planning a social gathering of some sort, she hosted many debates about politics or new scientific theories at her home. She also got involved with researching practicing medicine. Though women were not encouraged to write books or academic papers of any sort, Katherine published her own treatise, entitled *A Discourse on the Plague of 1665*.

THE STALBRIDGE YEARS

Boyle made many trips back to London, Oxford, and parts of England and Ireland over the next decade. But after fully coming into his inheritance in March 1646, he spent the majority of his time in Stalbridge—a 50-acre (20-ha) wooded estate surrounded by a stone wall. The fifth largest house in Dorset at the time, Stalbridge had majestic windows, dozens of tall chimneys sticking up from its roof, and plumbing throughout most of the rooms—a rarity at that time. Though the outside was crumbling in spots and some of the rooms were in disrepair, it was the perfect sanctuary for long walks with his spaniel and diving deep into his studies.

In contrast to the time he spent in London with Katherine, Boyle's years at Stalbridge were comparatively isolated.

> **I am grown so perfect a villager, and live so removed not only from the roads but from the very by-paths of intelligence, that to entertain you with our country discourse would have extremely puzzled me ... I could not have sent you so much as that of my being well,**

he wrote in a letter to a friend in London. But despite frequent bouts of melancholy, his solitude also left much time for thinking and writing. One of the first texts that Boyle worked on was a very ambitious 200-page paper entitled *The Aretology or Ethicall Elements*. In it, he attempted to define his own system of ethics. He explained how to live a virtuous and moral existence and explored the many obstacles that might stand in the way. Some of Boyle's other early projects included *Free Discourse Against Customary Swearing* and *The Dayly Reflection*, a treatise that discussed the benefits of keeping a daily journal. *Of the Study & Exposition of the Scriptures, Occasionall Mediations,* and *Scripture Observations* were three papers in which he reflected on scriptural passages from the Bible and advocated for the practice of exploring one's conscience on a regular basis.

Boyle also dabbled in writing fictional stories modeled after the popular French romances of the time period. In the mid-1640s, he wrote what eventually became *The Amorous Controversies*, a series of romantic stories structured as a correspondence between a man named Theophilus and his friend Lindamor. In each of the letters, Theophilus and Lindamor discuss the nature of love and how to properly woo a potential partner. Lindamor gripes about his failure to attract Hermione, the girl of his dreams, while Theophilus doles out helpful advice. In the series' final volume, eventually titled *Seraphic Love* and published in a revised edition in 1659, the letters recount the virtues of choosing spiritual love—a love of God—over pursuing earthly desires. Similar to Lindamor, Boyle was never successful in attracting a mate—not that he tried very hard. Instead, his reverence for religion—and, of course, science—became his soul's major pursuit during his lifetime.

THE INVISIBLE PHILOSOPHERS

Toward the end of the 1640s, Boyle was growing restless. Though the previous five years had been prolific ones and he researched projects or wrote nearly every day, his prospects for matrimony had dwindled. He settled into a life of celibacy.

To combat his loneliness, Boyle started hanging around with a group of influential mathematicians, scientists, and social reformers whose work he admired, including American alchemist George Starkey and Polish-born philosopher Samuel Hartlib. Hailing from Ireland, England, and abroad, the men called themselves the Invisible College. They held meetings at Gresham College in London and at University College in Oxford. At these gatherings, they debated hot topics of the day, such as Copernicus's heliocentric theories about the universe, Galileo's law of motion for falling bodies, and the mystery of comets. They gave each other homework, too. Books by Marin Mersenne, a French theologian who studied formulas involving prime numbers, and William Oughtred, an English

Marin Mersenne was a contemporary of the Invisible College's earliest members. Among other subjects, he studied pendulums, prime numbers, and theology.

MARIN MERSENNE

1588–1648

mathematician who made important discoveries in algebra and invented an early version of the slide rule, were among those in constant circulation.

Though he still spent most of his time alone, Boyle found the company of these men, when they found the time to get together, to be thrilling and inspiring. As he wrote in a letter to a friend in 1647,

> **The corner-stones of the invisible, or (as they term themselves) the philosophical college, do now and then honour me with their company … men of so capacious and searching spirits, that school-philosophy is but the lowest region of their knowledge.**

The work of Sir Francis Bacon, an English statesman and philosopher who came up with a scientific method for testing the truth of an idea by forming a hypothesis, then performing experiments to prove it correct or incorrect, was especially important to the group. In fact, it may have been Bacon's teachings that inspired Boyle to construct the first makeshift laboratory in his home from which he could carry out his own experiments. He filled it with beakers, test tubes, and even a microscope, which he used to observe the microcosmic structure of living things. He also installed a giant furnace for heating mineral substances to high tem-

Francis Bacon (1561–1626) is often described as the founder of the scientific method. His best-known work is his *Novum Organum* (*New Organon*). The title is a reference to Aristotle's *Organon*.

FRANCIS BACON: A MAN OF MANY TALENTS

Sir Francis Bacon was one of the most influential figures of the Scientific Revolution. He was the brain behind the scientific method. But before he was a scientist, Bacon was actually a statesman.

Francis Bacon was born on January 22, 1561, in London, England. Smart and a conscientious student at an early age, he graduated from Cambridge's Trinity College in 1575, when he was 14 years old. He then started law school but dropped out and moved to Paris to work under the British ambassador to France. In 1581, he landed a job in the House of Commons and went back to school to complete his law degree.

Bacon served in Parliament for nearly four decades, from 1584 to 1617. During that time, he moved up the ranks quickly and gained much recognition for his accomplishments. He became solicitor general in 1607 and attorney general in 1613. In 1618, he was appointed lord chancellor, one of the highest political offices in England. But in 1621, disaster struck. Bacon was accused of accepting bribes and was promptly impeached by Parliament for corruption. He was fined 40,000 pounds and sentenced to the Tower of London for imprisonment. Luckily, after serving only four days, his fine and sentence were reduced and he was released.

Despite the collapse of his political career, Bacon made an impact on society in other ways. As a philosopher interested in creating more informed ways to determine the truth of ideas, he devised the scientific method. This groundbreaking step-by-step inquiry process calls for asking a question about your topic first, then doing background research, proposing a hypothesis, conducting an experiment, and, finally, analyzing the results of your experiment to form conclusions.

Bacon died on April 9, 1626, after catching bronchitis during one of his experiments. Still, his work helped inform the Scientific Revolution and beyond.

peratures, so he could distill them down to determine their chemical properties.

During his Stalbridge period, Boyle conducted dozens, if not hundreds, of experiments. Under the tutelage of George Starkey, he studied alchemy—a field dedicated to transforming base metals into gold and figuring out which chemical substances can be used to prolong life. But despite his constant tinkering in his laboratory, Boyle felt the need for a change. Because of the near constant threat of war, the lengthy commute from Dorset to Oxford was treacherous and sometimes dangerous. To London, it was an even longer journey. Dorset was situated between London and the Southwest where much of the fighting was concentrated at that time. Consequently, Royalist and Parliamentarian armies were constantly passing through the area, making it difficult for locals to feel safe on their estates. At the start of a new decade, Boyle was ready to move on to the next phase of his life. It was time to find a new place to call home.

CHAPTER THREE

BOYLE'S BREAKTHROUGHS

Much like his return to England after his grand tour of Europe when he was a young teenager, 25-year-old Boyle emerged from his laboratory at Stalbridge Manor a changed man. At the turn of the new decade, the English Civil Wars were finally coming to an end. The Royalist army had been defeated in the Battle of Preston in 1648, and the king, Charles I, was subsequently executed in 1649.

That same year, Parliamentarian leader Oliver Cromwell set his sights on Ireland. He slaughtered the combined forces of the Irish Confederates and Royalists in the Battle of Drogheda. In May 1650, he led his army into Scotland, where Charles II—Charles I's son—was still considered the king. Cromwell defeated the Scots at the Battle of Dunbar on September 3, 1650.

Robert Boyle

After the English Civil Wars ended, Cromwell assumed power of England, Ireland, and Scotland in 1653. Instead of taking the title of "King," he opted for "Lord Protector."

Boyle's Breakthroughs

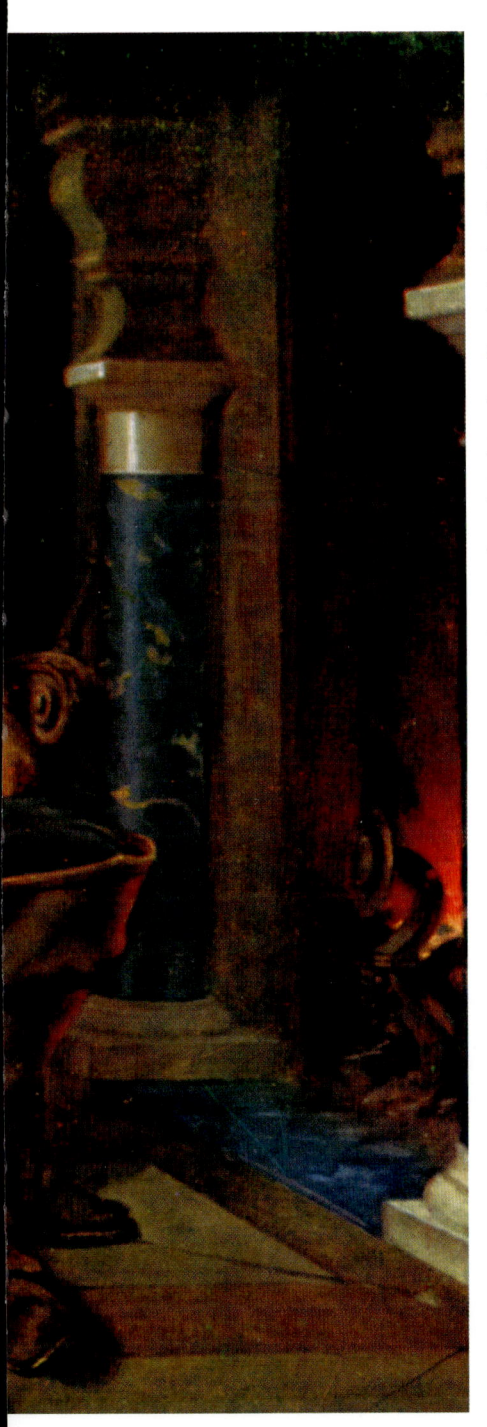

When Charles II and the Scots advanced back into England and Ireland in 1651, Cromwell was once again victorious. He crushed the Royalist army at the Battle of Worcester on September 3, effectively ending nine years of fighting in England. Not even a year later, in May 1652, the Irish city of Galway fell, too, putting a stop to Ireland's eleven-year war.

These developments on the world stage had a profound impact on Boyle, both mentally and financially. He left Stalbridge for Ireland to check in on a variety of properties he had inherited after his father's death. Because many of the Irish were forced to relinquish control of their properties to English colonists after the war, Boyle gained a considerable amount of land and money. His new assets and incoming rent meant he was extraordinarily wealthy. From that point forward, he was able to pursue his scientific interests full time without the need to earn money.

Despite his financial windfall, Boyle's two years in Ireland were marred by tragedy. He endured a series of debilitating accidents and ailments, including a nasty fall from a horse, a case of dropsy (a swelling beneath the skin that causes severe pain), and a terrible fever that left him close to blind. As a result, he would need others to read for him and transcribe his notes for the rest of his life. At the end of this last illness, Boyle contacted his sister Katherine to ask for her help once again. Through her social and political connections, she secured two rooms for her brother in a house in Oxford.

OXFORD AND THE ROYAL SOCIETY

As 1656 got underway, Boyle began settling into his new life. Oxford was a university town and offered him much access to a furnace, beakers, and other tools with which to set up his new laboratory. More importantly, Boyle was now in closer proximity to many of the like-minded scholars he knew from earlier Invisible College meetings who were just as interested in pushing the boundaries of science and knowledge as he was.

There were men like John Wilkins, who was the head of Wadham College (part of Oxford University) and who later briefly served as master of Trinity College

A member of Boyle's Invisible College, John Wallis was also one of the most influential mathematicians of the Scientific Revolution. He contributed to the development of calculus.

at Cambridge. Other Oxford teachers included John Wallis, professor of geometry, and Seth Ward, professor of astronomy. Christopher Wren, who succeeded Ward as professor of astronomy in 1661, was a member, too. Wren eventually went on to design a number of important buildings throughout England, including St. Paul's Cathedral in London, the Royal Observatory at Greenwich, and Trinity College Library in Cambridge.

As in meetings of past years, each of these men contributed their own ideas about the study of natural philosophy, a way of examining the physical world through a philosophical lens. They read scholarly texts by Pierre Gassendi, a French astronomer and mathematician who was the first scientist to observe the planet Mercury's movement across the Sun. They also latched on to and debated many of the theories posited by René Descartes, a French philosopher. Among other things, Descartes sought to uncover the meaning of the natural world using a rational approach—through math and science—and became famous for his statement, "I think; therefore I am."

By the turn of the decade, Boyle and the rest of the members of the Invisible College were getting together regularly to discuss their latest findings, often at Boyle's Oxford lodgings. Following a lecture by Christopher Wren at Gresham College in London, they decided to make their organization official. On

Boyle's Breakthroughs

November 28, 1660, they formed the Royal Society, headquartered in London but with chapters in Oxford and elsewhere throughout England. Two years later, the group was given a Royal Charter by Charles II, signaling his official approval.

THE ROYAL SOCIETY: A LOOK INTO THE FUTURE

Officially formed in 1660, the Royal Society has become one of the world's most esteemed organizations dedicated to the advancement of scientific thought. Its publication, *Philosophical Transactions*, is the oldest continuously published science journal in the world. Today, there are more than 1,600 members from different countries across the globe who have followed in the footsteps of former members such as Isaac Newton, Charles Darwin, Albert Einstein, and Robert Boyle. Here are just a few modern Royal Society members:

Stephen Hawking: A theoretical physicist who has made groundbreaking contributions to the study of gravity and the origins of the universe. He proposed that the Big Bang was the inevitable con-

(CONTINUED ON THE NEXT PAGE)

sequence of the laws of physics, rather than an act of God. He also came up with a set of laws governing black holes.

Dame Jocelyn Bell Burnell: An astrophysicist who discovered pulsars, rotating neutron stars that appear to "pulse," as the beam of light they emit can only be seen when it faces Earth. Burnell's work is widely considered to be one of the greatest astronomical findings of the twentieth century.

Sir Venki Ramakrishnan: A structural biologist who was awarded the Nobel Prize in Chemistry in 2009 for his work on the structures of ribosomes, cellular machines that synthesize protein in living organisms. He was also knighted by the British government in 2012, an honor given to individuals signifying their place in the Most Excellent Order of the British Empire.

Dorothy Hodgkin: A biochemist who became the first woman appointed to be a Royal Society Fellow on March 20, 1947. In 1964, she became the first British woman to win the Nobel Prize.

EXPERIMENTS WITH A VACUUM

The Royal Society's official motto was *Nullius in verba*, which can be roughly translated to "Take nobody's word for it." Like many of the group's members, Boyle took the statement very seriously. Over the next 30 years, he used the idea to fuel new experiments. Toward the end of the 1650s, Boyle met an Oxford University student named Robert Hooke. Hooke was born on July 18, 1635, in the town of Freshwater on the Isle of Wight, in the English Channel. He would eventually go on to do important work in a wide array of fields, including astronomy, chemistry, geometry, and physics. However, he is best known today for his work in biology. In 1665 he published a book called *Micrographia*, which featured incredibly detailed drawings of living things—such as plants and insects—many of which were examined using a variety of magnifying lenses. It was in this volume that Hooke used the word "cell" to describe the walled compartments he saw inside a piece of cork. He chose the name because the shapes of the units reminded him of the small rooms—called *cellula*—in which monks lived. We now know that all living things are composed of cells.

Hooke was so intelligent and skilled at working with mechanical equipment that Boyle hired him as his laboratory assistant. The partnership between the two men grew to be especially fruitful. Boyle and Hooke started working with the first vacuum pump, invented by German scientist Otto von Guericke in 1650. After Hooke improved upon its design, he and Boyle used the contraption to create a vacuum and conducted various experiments.

What they discovered was extraordinary. Using the scientific method by coming up with a set of hypotheses and then engaging in a series of tests to confirm or deny each claim, Boyle and Hooke determined the properties of air. First, they placed a bell inside a glass jar. Then, they used a magnet attached to the outside of the jar to ring the bell. Finally, they used a crank at the bottom of the jar to activate the vacuum. As air was sucked out from the top, the sound of the bell diminished, but the light from the room trapped inside the jar remained constant. This experiment proved a number of hypotheses to be true. First, light can travel through a vacuum, but sound cannot. Second, as demonstrated

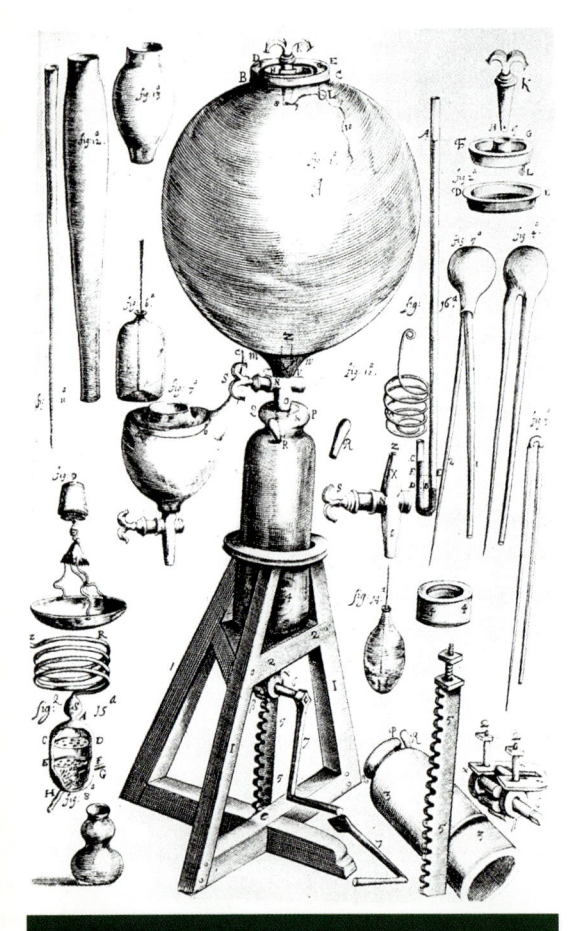

This drawing of Boyle and Hooke's vacuum pump is from Boyle's *New Experiments Physico-Mechanical, Touching the Spring of the Air, and Its Effects.*

Boyle's Breakthroughs

by the magnet's effect on the bell, physical forces can move through a vacuum.

Robert Boyle created many experiments using air pump technology. In the one depicted here, he discovered that sound cannot travel in a vacuum.

Thrilled with their results, Boyle and Hooke did more tests. They lit a candle inside the jar. As in the previous experiment with the bell, they created a vacuum. As the air was pulled out of the jar, the flame shrunk smaller and smaller until it finally burned out. This showed them that fire needs air.

BOYLE'S LAW

The discoveries Boyle and Hooke made about air inside a vacuum had a huge impact on how scientists thought about the physical world. But perhaps the most far-reaching breakthrough was the duo's research on the relationship between pressure and volume. In one experiment, they took a J-shaped glass tube and filled it partially with mercury; the other part of the tube was filled with air. Then, they used the vacuum pump to exert pressure on the tube by forcing the air inside downward. What happened as a result proved that when pressure on a gas—air—is increased, the gas's volume shrinks in a proportional way.

Boyle reported these initial findings in a 1660 paper entitled *New Experiments Physico-Mechanical, Touching the Spring of the Air, and Its Effects*. After receiving criticism from some of his contemporaries regarding his methods and the conclusions he drew, he went back to his laboratory and did more experiments. In 1662,

NEW EXPERIMENTS

PHYSICO-MECHANICAL,

Touching

The Spring of the Air, and its Effects,

Made, for the most part, in a New

Pnuematical Engine,

Written by way of LETTER

To the Right Honorable CHARLES Lord

Vicount of DUNGARVAN,

Eldest Son to the Earl of CORKE.

By the Honorable ROBERT BOYLE Esq;

LONDON,

Printed by *Miles Flesher* for *Richard Davis*, Bookseller in

Boyle's New Experiments Physico-Mechanical, Touching the Spring of the Air, and Its Effects put him squarely on the map as a prominent thinker of the times.

Boyle published a revised second edition. In it, he proposed that the volume of a gas is inversely proportional to the pressure being exerted upon it, as long as the temperature doesn't change. This idea later became known as Boyle's law.

To understand Boyle's law in terms of everyday life, think of what happens in the lungs. First, take a breath in. The lungs expand and the diaphragm contracts. The pressure inside the lungs decreases. Now exhale. The diaphragm relaxes upward and the volume of the lungs decreases, while the pressure inside them increases.

Here is another example of Boyle's law in action. Think of flying in an airplane. As the plane ascends into the air, it travels from an area of high pressure on the ground, which humans' ears are accustomed to, to an area of low pressure. As a result of the change in altitude, the air inside the ear struggles to adjust to the air outside the ear. Pressure on the eardrum is increased, and pain is possible. But swallowing or yawning allows the ear to "pop" and the pressure to escape. Relief arrives when pressure in the ear

Boyle's Breakthroughs

is released. The volume of the air is inversely proportional to the pressure being exerted upon it.

Today, Boyle's law is taken as fact. But back when he was conducting these experiments, Boyle and many other scientists during the Scientific Revolution were ridiculed for going against the teachings of Aristotle and the church. Consequently, they made sure to document

Boyle's law was discovered more than 300 years ago. But the rules still apply. The theory explains why your ears "pop" on an airplane as you ascend and descend.

each discovery by taking copious notes and writing lengthy papers explaining their findings. This way, any naysayer or colleague could replicate their efforts or build upon them to conduct further studies.

Boyle's *New Experiments*, as the paper is often called, made waves when the revised edition was published in 1662. But it wasn't the only project he was working on at the time. Over the next decade, Boyle produced a wealth of information that changed the course of scientific history. His new focus: chemistry.

CHAPTER FOUR

THE FATHER OF CHEMISTRY

As the 1660s progressed, the inaugural members of the Royal Society continued to be enthralled by all manners of research and experimentation—increasingly becoming the backbone of the Scientific Revolution. As Flora Masson wrote in her 1914 biography of Boyle,

> There was really no form of 'curiosity' of earth, or sea, or sky, that was not grist to the Gresham College mill. Chariots and watches, masonry, ores, 'the nature of salts,' injection into the veins and the transfusion of blood, the velocity of bullets, mine-damp, musical sounds and instruments, thermometers and barometers, fossils, shooting stars, and double keels were all mixed up in most admired disorder.

Robert Boyle

The Royal Society held meetings at Gresham College in London until 1710. Gresham College provided free lectures to Londoners in the former home of Sir Thomas Gresham.

The Father of Chemistry

References to places in the College.

1. Gate into Bishopsgate street.
2. Court within the gate.
3. Physic prof. lodgings.
4. Reading hall.
5. Music prof. lodgings. Porters rooms underneath.
6. Passage between the two courts
7. Green court.
8. Observatory.
9. Geometry prof. lodgings.
10. Back door into the geometry prof. lodgings.
11. Room behind the reading hall.
12. Divinity prof. lodgings.
13. Physic prof. elaboratory.
14. Back door to the elaboratory.
15. Rhetoric prof. lodgings.
16. Door into the rhetoric prof. lodgings.
17. North piazza.
18. Astronomy prof. lodgings
19. South or long gallery.
20. South piazza.
21. Fore door into the astronomy prof. lodgings.
22. West or white gallery.
23. Almes houses.
24. West end of the south gallery.
25. Gate into the stable yard.
26. Law prof. lodgings.
27. Fore door into the law prof. lodgings.
28. Passage into Sun yard.
29. Stable yard and stables.

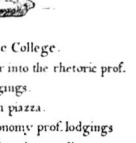

The London faction at Gresham College elected a secretary, Henry Oldenburg, who took notes during each Royal Society meeting and sent them to colleagues scattered farther afield in Oxford and elsewhere. Oldenburg penned many letters to Boyle containing London's most pressing gossip. He also described the attention the society was getting around the globe, from France, Germany, and Italy, to Poland, New England, and even the East Indies.

As Oldenburg kept track of goings-on in London, Boyle stayed busy in Oxford, working on his projects with gusto. Because of the society's increased influence, he was more determined than ever to get his scientific discoveries down on paper. He published his works in both Latin and English so interested parties around the world could read them. Between 1660 and

1666, Boyle wrote an astonishing 12 books. That's an average of 140,000 words per year!

A REVISED APPROACH TO SCIENCE

By the mid-1600s, the Scientific Revolution was evolving at a rapid pace. In order to keep up and make his mark on the movement, Boyle often had multiple manuscripts in the works at any given time. With *New Experiments Physico-Mechanical, Touching the Spring of the Air and Its Effects* hot off the press, he produced two more important books in 1661. The first, *Certain Physiological Essays and Other Tracts*, consisted of a series of essays that, among other things, defined how to best conduct a proper experiment and record the results.

One of the most valuable ideas presented in the book was the notion that unsuccessful experiments should be repeated and carefully documented in great detail, not ignored. How else, Boyle argued, could scientists improve upon each other's work if they weren't made aware of past failures? In some cases as well, scientists doing the same experiment might get different outcomes. Boyle argued that all information and details—not just the positive results—were important. As he wrote in the essay entitled "Of Unsucceeding Experiments," "even when we find not what we seek, we find something as well worth seeking as what we missed."

Boyle conducted hundreds of experiments over the course of his lifetime. But he didn't do it alone. He often employed laboratory assistants to help him with his work and take notes on his findings.

When *Certain Physiological Essays* was published, many scientists championed Boyle's theories and vowed to use his methods going forward.

> [He] was an experimenter par excellence, both in theory and practice. Though Francis Bacon may have laid down guidelines for the pursuit of inductive science by controlled experiment, it was Boyle who worked out such ideas in full, eclectically building on precedents provided not only by Bacon, but also by other traditions,

wrote Michael Hunter in *Robert Boyle: An Introduction*. In fact, it was Boyle's meticulous approach to experimentation and resulting self-confidence that inspired him to forge a path into a new area of scientific study later known as chemistry.

CHEMISTRY IS BORN

Many historic texts and biographies, refer to Boyle is as the father of chemistry—for good reason. When he was living in Oxford, he grew increasingly obsessed with figuring out the elemental makeup of the objects he encountered in daily life. In medieval times, most scientists did so by following either Aristotle's teachings or those of the Swiss-German doctor Paracelsus.

Paracelsus's research on metals led to his reputation as the father of toxicology. He is also responsible for many of the earliest discoveries in chemotherapy, a treatment for cancer.

WHO WERE THE ALCHEMISTS?

Prior to what is now known as chemistry, there was a different method to discerning the nature of the universe: alchemy. Today, an often-cited fact is that one of alchemists' main goals was to turn metal into gold. While this might be true, it is worth understanding *why* they wanted to do so, as well as other aspects of their ancient belief system, which still exists in a different form to this day.

During the Middle Ages, alchemy was quite a secretive field. Its followers thought that objects had a universal spirit and that metals were alive and held magical properties. Perhaps the most defining symbol of alchemy was its followers' belief in the existence of the philosopher's stone. Not a literal rock, the philosopher's stone was thought to be a type of powder. Applying it to a base metal, such as lead, would transform the metal into gold, its most perfect form. Alchemists also believed the philosopher's stone could be used as an "elixir of life." Its transformative healing powers could bring about immortality.

Alchemy has gone through many evolutions throughout its existence. Some alchemists divided nature into four main regions—the warm, the cold, the moist, and the dry—in order to understand the universe. Others identified each piece of matter as male or female in order to understand its true essence. Today, there is even an International Alchemy Guild headquartered in Colorado. According to the organization's website, the IAG's philosophy is based on three principles taken from ancient practices: "The universe is striving toward perfection. Consciousness is a force in nature. All is one."

Aristotle believed that matter was composed of four elements: earth, fire, water, and air. Take the example of a tree stump. If heated, wood will burn (fire), release moisture (water) and smoke (air), and leave behind a pile of ash (earth). In contrast, Paracelsus, like many alchemists, alleged that the universe was made up of metals that took various forms in different states. Paracelsus believed that all matter was composed of not four, but three key elements: sulfur, mercury, and salt. These three ingredients could also be used to treat certain diseases, such as syphilis.

Though Boyle admired the alchemists whose beliefs gained traction during the Middle Ages, he didn't agree with either Aristotle's or Paracelsus's theories.

Instead, he offered up his own alternatives in the second text he published in 1661, *The Sceptical Chymist*. The book was structured as a dialogue between four characters. Themistius relayed Aristotle's point of view, while Philoponus represented Paracelsus. The two other characters were Carneades, the "skeptical chemist" of the title, and Eleutherius, the open-minded listener.

The book unfolds much like a lecture given by Carneades, clearly a stand-in for Boyle. Carneades argues that the Aristotelian four-element system and the Paracelsian three-principle model are wrong. In their place, he suggests that elements are simple substances that cannot disintegrate into other substances and that compounds are created when elements combine to form new substances.

Secondly, Boyle proposes that bodies are made up of atoms or necessary particles. Chemistry, or the study of the behavior of substances, can be explained through the motion of these atoms. Lastly, he argues that all substances fit into three basic categories: alkaline, acidic, or neutral. He came up with this idea after mixing chemical substances and vegetable dyes together and monitoring the results. For example, acids turn blue vegetable solutions red, while neutral solutions do not. This—and, thus, *The Sceptical Chymist*—was a crucial step toward the future development of reliable pH indicators in chemistry.

THE SCEPTICAL CHYMIST:
OR CHYMICO-PHYSICAL
Doubts & Paradoxes,

Touching the
SPAGYRIST'S PRINCIPLES
Commonly call'd
HYPOSTATICAL,
As they are wont to be Propos'd and
Defended by the Generality of
ALCHYMISTS.

Whereunto is præmis'd Part of another Discourse relating to the same Subject.

BY
The Honourable ROBERT BOYLE, Esq;

LONDON,
Printed by *J. Cadwell* for *J. Crooke*, and are to be Sold at the *Ship* in St. *Paul's* Church-Yard.
MDCLXI.

In *The Sceptical Chymist,* Boyle argued against Aristotle's and Paracelsus's theories on matter in order to advance his own ideas about chemistry.

A NEW IMAGE

By the time he had reached his mid-30s, Boyle's world—and influence—had grown exponentially from the days of being holed up in Stalbridge, waiting to set up his first laboratory. Thanks, in part, to the profound contributions he had already made to the advancement of science as illustrated in *Certain Physiological Essays* and *The Sceptical Chymist*, he began to enjoy recognition among his peers. More scientists in other far-flung countries became aware of his work and wanted to find out more about what he was working on. Boyle was ready for the challenge.

After years of having to dictate his manuscripts to scribes, then repeat the process if a second edition was warranted, Boyle came up with a new way of editing his manuscripts. He wrote on separate leaves of paper, then actually cut and pasted the various versions together during the revision process. Before long, his output increased. He published a number of new texts, including *Some Considerations Touching the Usefulness of Experimental Natural Philosophy* (1663, 1671), *Experiments and Considerations Touching Colours* (1664), *New Experiments and Observations Touching Cold* (1665), *Experimental History of Chemistry* (1665), *Hydrostatical Paradoxes* (1666), and *The Origine of Formes and Qualities* (1666).

It was during this period of increased productivity that Boyle commissioned his first portrait in 1664. As

THE FATHER OF CHEMISTRY

BRRR! BOYLE'S EXPERIMENTS WITH COLD

The winter of 1664 brought ferocious winds and massive snowstorms to Oxford. Sensing a perfect opportunity, Boyle began conducting experiments to find out how various gases, solids, and liquids reacted in subfreezing conditions. In addition, he interviewed people who had firsthand experience dealing with extreme temperatures—Hudson Bay

(CONTINUED ON THE NEXT PAGE)

Through copious experiments in frigid weather, Boyle disproved Aristotle's theory that heated water freezes faster than water at room temperature.

(CONTINUED FROM THE PREVIOUS PAGE)

Company sea captains and Samuel Collins, the physician to the czar of Russia. The result was *New Experiments and Observations Touching Cold*, published in 1665.

The book was notable for a number of reasons. Each set of ideas was arranged under a thematic title. Examples include "Experiments Touching Bodies Capable of Freezing Others," "Experiments and Observations Touching the Duration of Ice and Snow, and the Destroying of Them by the Air, and Several Liquors," and "Experiments and Observations of the Preservation and Destruction of (Eggs, Apples, and Other) Bodies by Cold."

Boyle also paid particular attention to describing the tools he used in each experiment, especially new types of alcohol thermometers. He included pictures, diagrams, and graphs. A detailed list of sources he used was added as well, in case other scientists wanted to fact check his work or use the resources in their own experiments.

Finally, with the publication of *New Experiments and Observations Touching Cold*, Boyle proposed many concepts that we take for granted today. He explored the benefits of using cold storage to preserve food. He was also thrilled to report that water expands when it freezes.

was common practice, the 37-year-old hired a renowned painter to do the job. Dressed in a regal cloak and white lace cravat, he sat in front of a curtain while William Faithorne painstakingly reproduced Boyle's image on parchment paper. Later that same year, Faithorne produced an engraved version of the drawing, per Boyle's request.

Unlike most portraits at the time, which often showed their subjects in front of a landscape backdrop, at a desk, or seated in a chair, Faithorne's engraving of Boyle was strikingly different. Instead of a nature scene in the background, Boyle's vacuum pump—his first claim to fame, which led to the discovery of Boyle's law—was prominently featured.

CHAPTER FIVE

From Science to Salvation: The London Chapter

In the summer of 1665, a pall had fallen over London. Earlier that May, parishioners of St. Giles-in-the-Fields, a parish outside the city, started falling ill. They had been bitten by fleas carried on the backs of rats. The bites caused large black welts on the churchgoers' legs and oozing sores on their necks. One by one, nearly 50 of them died after days of agonizing fever and vomiting.

The bubonic plague had broken out and was spreading like wildfire. Houses filled with the afflicted were marked by a painted red cross and the words, "Lord have mercy on us!" on the door. At night, corpses were dragged out, piled into a cart, and dumped into giant pits overflowing with dead bodies and buzzing flies. In July of that year, 17,036 Londoners perished. In August, 31,159 more succumbed to the disease. By

From Science to Salvation: The London Chapter

the end of the summer, nearly 69,000 deaths—roughly 15 percent of London's population—were officially recorded. It was the worst plague outbreak in England since 1348.

While Boyle was safe in Oxford, Hooke and other members of the Royal Society were not. They, along with Charles II and the rest of the royal family, relocated from London to other parts of England. Between June 28, 1665, and February 21, 1666, no

Published in *The Intelligencer* newspaper on June 26, 1665, this illustration shows the angel of death gazing out over London during the plague epidemic.

official meetings were held by the Royal Society. Oxford became the temporary seat of government until London could be declared free of disease.

When the weather got colder and temperatures dropped below zero, killing the fleas, plague cases dwindled. But London still wasn't immune to disaster. On September 1, 1666, Charles II's baker failed to properly extinguish a fire in his oven at home. The next morning, the smoldering ashes caught and ignited a pile of twigs against a neighboring wall. Like many buildings in London at the time, the baker's home was made mostly of wood. It burst into flames.

Soon the blustery winds pushed the fire across the street and into a stable filled with hay. From there it spread to a group of warehouses packed with coal, candles, lamp oil, and liquor, causing a giant inferno that spread far and wide. By September 6 when the raging blaze was finally put out, approximately 13,000 houses and 90 churches had been destroyed across London. Nearly 100,000 people were left homeless.

Despite the destruction of the great city, only 16 people are recorded as having lost their lives. As soon as they were able, members of the Royal Society helped pick up the rubble. Christopher Wren designed the new St. Paul's Cathedral. Robert Hooke—newly appointed professor of geometry at Gresham College, London, and Wren's chief assistant—helped create a monument that

From Science to Salvation: The London Chapter

In September 1666, the Great Fire swept across London, destroying thousands of homes and buildings in its path, including the old St. Paul's Cathedral.

commemorated the Great Fire. It told the story of what transpired that fateful September day in 1666.

Luckily Boyle's sister Katherine, and her house,

WHAT IS CORPUSCULARIANISM?

As the Great Fire was raging in London in 1666, Boyle was tinkering in his laboratory in Oxford. That same year, he published *The Origine of Formes and Qualities*. In it, he described his theory for the way the world worked. As Pierre Gassendi and René Descartes discussed in their earlier works and Boyle touched upon in *The Sceptical Chymist*, Boyle believed that everything could be explained in terms of the interaction of matter and motion. He called this his "corpuscular" hypothesis.

According to Boyle, corpuscularianism states that all matter is composed of tiny "corpuscles," or particles. Each of these particles has a shape, size, and type of motion. In order to learn the properties of a material, scientists must study the combinations and collisions of its corpuscles. For example, to figure out how a substance might dissolve in a solvent, Boyle suggested paying attention to the way its particles moved and interacted with each other in space.

remained unharmed. With his finances still in good shape, Robert sent her money to distribute to those in need. Katherine was grateful.

I have since taken to myself the mortification of seeing the desolations that God, in his just and dreadful judgment, has made in the poor City, which is thereby now turned indeed into a ruinous heap, and gave me the most amazing spectacle that I have ever beheld in my progress about and into this ruin,

she wrote in a letter to Robert. "I dispensed your Charity amongst some poor families and persons that I found yet in the fields unhoused."

A MOVE TO LONDON

By the end of 1667, Boyle's relationship with Oxford was on a downswing. Many of the philosophers with whom he had collaborated since moving there a decade prior had left for London. Robert also missed Katherine, whom he had always adored.

In 1668, he again picked up shop and moved in with Katherine in central London. Her house on Pall Mall was near the royal court and St. James' Park, lush gardens that Charles II restored and filled with exotic animals and birds. In fact, her residence was so close that the king would occasionally pop by to ask Robert's opinion on scientific matters.

Robert had a suite of rooms at Pall Mall—a large bedroom, an entertaining area, and, of course, his precious laboratory filled with the latest equipment. The house was as lively as it was when he lived there as a boy of 17. There were often so many visitors that Boyle had to restrict his socializing so he could continue to focus on his experiments. During his first two years there, he published two works: *A Continuation of New Experiments Physico-Mechanical, Touching the Spring and Weight of the Air, and Their Effects* and *Tracts about the Cosmicall Qualities of Things, the Temperature of the Subterraneal and Submarine Regions, the Bottom of the Sea, &c. with an Introduction to the History of Particular Qualities.*

Under Katherine's wing again and in the direct

The English monarchy was restored under Charles II, who was the king of Great Britain and Ireland from 1660 until his death in 1685.

company of Hooke and Oldenburg, Boyle's life was going swimmingly. But in the summer of 1670, he had a small stroke, which left him temporarily paralyzed.

> I have taken so many medicines and found the relief they awarded me so slow, that it is not easy for me to tell you what I found most good by ... I seldom missed a day without taking the air, at least once, and that even when I was at the weakest, and was fain to be carried in men's arms from my chair to the couch ... that the best thing I found to strengthen my feet and legs, which I still use, was sack turned to a brine with sea-salt and well rubbed upon the parts every morning and night with a warm hand,

he wrote in a letter to his friend in Dorset, John Mallet.

Boyle's health recovered slowly. Though pale and withered physically, he never stopped working. His illness sparked an interest in medicine and prompted a new wave of experiments in the laboratory. Over the next decade, Boyle published more than ten books and treatises, including *Tracts Consisting of Observations about the Saltness of the Sea* (1673), *Tracts: Containing Suspicions about Some Hidden Qualities of the Air* (1674), and *Observations upon an Artificial Substance That Shines Without Any Preceding Illustration* (1678).

A TURN TO GOD

After Boyle turned 46 in 1673, and perhaps because of his brush with mortality, his focus started to shift. Of course, he was still as interested in the science of matter, motion, and chemistry as ever. But he also made an effort to publish more treatises about religion, God, and human consciousness. More specifically, he viewed his theological interests and his work in science as interconnected. He used experimental results from one to inform matters in the other. In 1674 and 1675, he published *The Excellency of Theology, Compar'd with Natural Philosophy* and *Some Considerations about the Reconcileableness of Reason and Religion.* These two important works defined his religious and philosophical beliefs as an interrelated whole. In them, he discussed weighty matters such as whether reincarnation was possible in plants or bodies, how to live a pure Christian life and avoid sin, and the limitations of human intellect and reason when compared to the omniscience of God.

As the director of the East India Company and the Society for the Propagation of the Gospel, Boyle was active in pushing his Christian beliefs onto others. He paid large sums to have the Bible translated into different languages specifically for that purpose. "To convert Infidels to the Christian Religion is a work of great Charity and kindnes to men," he wrote at that

FROM SCIENCE TO SALVATION: THE LONDON CHAPTER

AN INFLUENTIAL POST

In 1669, Boyle was elected director of the East India Company, an English company that organized and handled imports and exports of exotic goods from the Far East. This position introduced Boyle to many fascinating and influential people around the world. It also allowed him access to valuable stones like diamonds, which informed his research for his 1672 treatise, *An Essay about the Origine and Virtues of Gems.*

But there was another side of the East India Company that particularly interested Boyle. Because of his firm Christian beliefs, he supported the company's mission to convert "poor infidels" from countries in which they did business. He felt it was their moral obligation to do so. Boyle donated large amounts of his own money to the company to fuel the missionaries' progress.

time. It frees them from "the gross errors and prejudices they had entertain'd before they were instructed in it [and] the vices and polutions they securely liv'd in, before they receiv'd the Gospel."

By 1680, Boyle's focus on looking inward had

Robert Boyle

The East India Company's first headquarters were located on Leadenhall Street in London. The majestic building was torn down in 1726. Today an office building stands in its place.

caused his participation in Royal Society meetings to dwindle. He was appointed president of the organization but declined the honor. According to his biographer Michael Hunter, Boyle did so because though he still believed in the Royal Society's mission, he objected to taking oaths on principle. Christopher Wren was elected instead.

Over the next ten years, Boyle continued to examine religion and its role in science and rational thought. He published *A Discourse of Things above Reason, Inquiring Whether a Philosopher Should Admit There Are Any Such* (1681); *Of the High Veneration Man's Intellect Owes to God, Peculiarly for his Wisedome and Power* (1685); *A Disquisition about the Final Causes of Natural Things* (1688), and *The Christian Virtuoso* (1690), among other papers. But as he aged and his body became frailer, his rapid-fire publishing schedule diminished. Still, he never completely stopped tinkering in his laboratory. In the last decade of his life, his dedication to science and uncovering answers to the universe's most puzzling questions was as strong as ever.

CHAPTER SIX

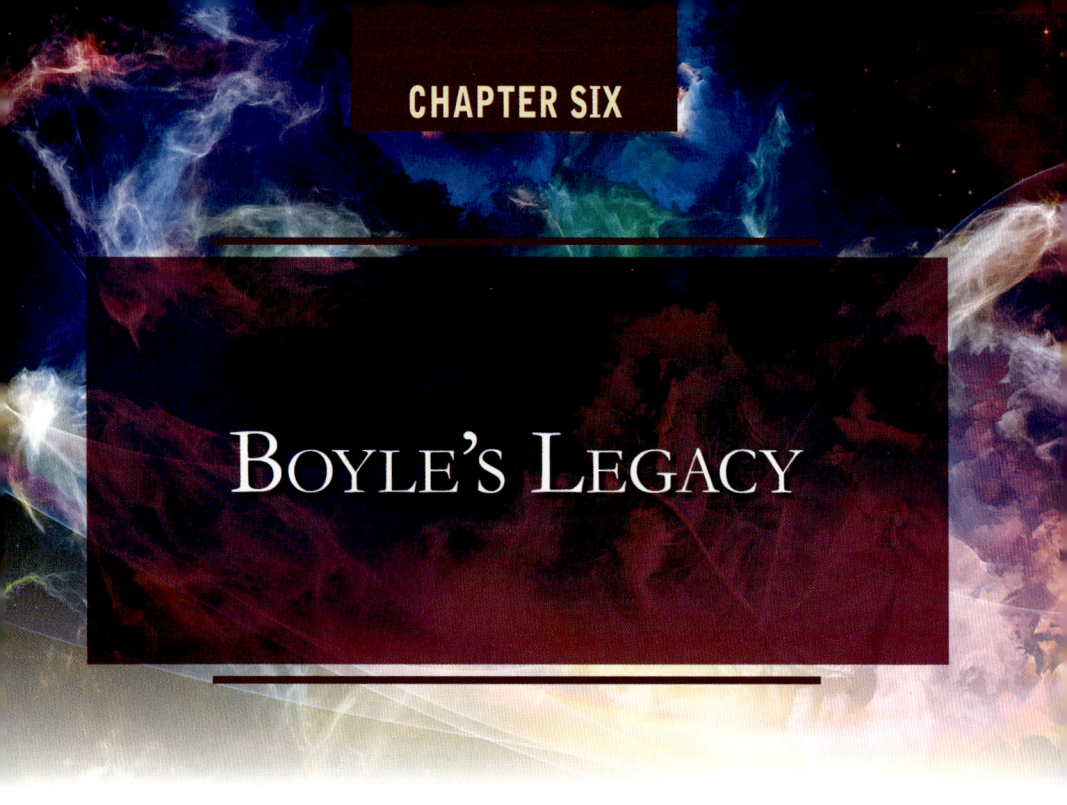

Boyle's Legacy

It was 1690—ten years before a new century began. The world had come a long way since the days of believing that Earth was the center of the universe and that planets revolved around it in circular motions. Thanks to men like Francis Bacon, René Descartes, Robert Hooke, and Christopher Wren, mathematics and reason were now an integral part of scientific study.

After the death of Copernicus in 1543 and Galileo in 1642, new brilliant thinkers had taken center stage. Scientist and mathematician Isaac Newton broke new ground in the study of planetary motion, light, and gravity. His *Philosophiae Naturalis Principia Mathematica* (*Mathematical Principles of Natural Philosophy*) was, perhaps, the single most influential book on physics published during this period. In addition to other ideas, the *Principia*, as it is usu-

Boyle's Legacy

ally called, described the three major rules of motion. One: An object will remain stationary unless it comes in contact with an external force. Two: Force is equal to mass multiplied by acceleration; a change in motion is proportional to the amount of force placed on an object. And, three: For every action, there is an equal and opposite reaction.

John Locke was another key player in the latter days of the Scientific Revolution. He investigated philosophical matters of the mind and soul in his work. His views influenced many scientific thinkers like Boyle who were grappling with the cross-pollination of science and religion, reason and faith. In 1689, Locke published his *An Essay Concerning Human Understanding*, which discussed the nature of identity and selfhood. Locke thought that gaining knowledge

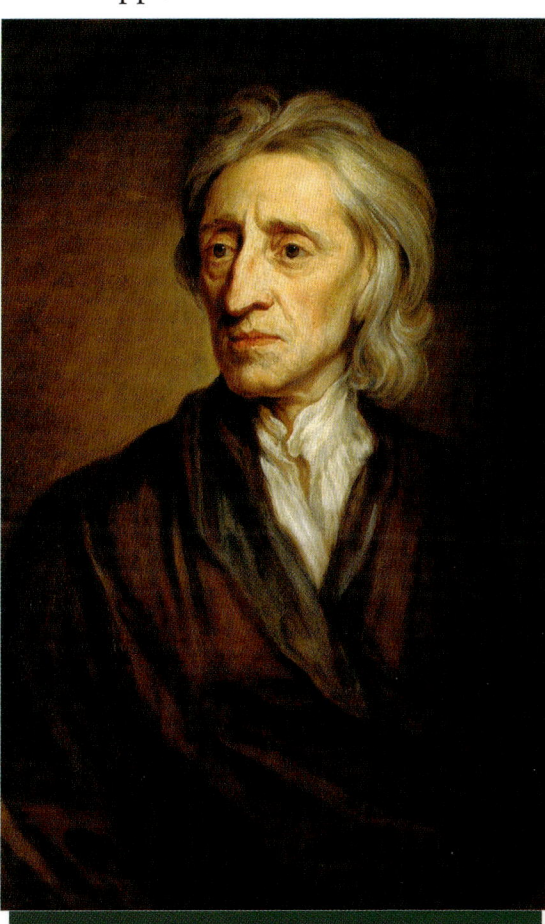

Along with his writings on the nature of the self, John Locke's essays on religious tolerance provided a model for the separation of church and state.

meant acquiring facts based on sensory experience. He advocated using the scientific method and experimentation to discover these truths.

Around that same time, Boyle enlisted Locke's help on a paper to be titled *History of the Air*. But he was also involved in his own solo project, this one addressing medicine. Picking up where he had left off in the 1660s with his work in progress, *Considerations & Doubts Touching the Vulgar Method of Physick*, Boyle ramped up his attack on Galenic therapy, also known as humorism.

Influenced by Aristotelian thought, humorism was the dominant theory in Europe for many centuries. Its proponents believed the human body was made up four humors, or liquids: blood, black bile, yellow bile, and phlegm. Each humor was associated with one of Aristotle's fundamental elements—air, water, earth, and fire—as well as a particular season of the year and a temperature. In order to remain healthy in body and mind, humorists believed that a person should have a good balance between the four humors. Any imbalance could result in disease. Treatments for illness involved exercise, herbal medicines, or dietary adjustments. More severe methods included searing the skin with a hot iron or bloodletting.

Boyle was staunchly opposed to humorism. He claimed that many of its suggested treatments were harmful rather than helpful. The practice of bloodletting was

This seventeenth-century engraving shows a woman having blood let. Bloodletting was a common practice for treating diseases during the Scientific Revolution.

especially damaging, for example. It weakened patients rather than giving them the much-needed strength they lacked and left them open to more serious illnesses.

Despite these firm objections, Boyle never completed the paper. Though he touched on similar ideas in *Medicina Hydrostatica*, which was published in 1690, he declined to take a firm stance on whether Galenic therapy could cause serious damage. Maybe it was the kindness of doctors who had treated him in the past that prevented him from speaking out against the common practice. Or perhaps it was his steadily aging body and weakened state that kept his lips sealed. Either way, Boyle's days of publishing groundbreaking theories about the latest developments in medicine, philosophy, and science were shrinking in number.

PREPARING FOR THE END

At the onset of 1691, Boyle's life was winding down and he knew it. In the last six years, he had witnessed Charles I's surviving son, James II, take control of the throne in England, Ireland, and Scotland, after Charles II died. Then, during the Glorious Revolution of 1688, Boyle watched James II's son-in-law William of Orange take over the job with James II's daughter Mary as queen. Boyle once again occasionally served as a scientific advisor, especially to William and Mary.

Located on the ceiling of the Painted Hall at Royal Naval College in London, this portrait celebrates the succession of William III and Mary II to the throne during the Glorious Revolution of 1688.

LOST PAPERS!

Boyle published dozens of papers over the course of his life. He took hundreds, if not thousands of pages of notes and worked on many drafts of his manuscripts before their publication. Then in May 1688, the unthinkable happened. Some of his papers got lost—or, at least, he claimed they did.

He published an advertisement written by one of his assistants. The advertisement stated that Boyle couldn't find some of his most important work journals. When they suddenly appeared later on, Boyle maintained that they had indeed been taken, but that the thief must have returned them after feeling remorse.

On the heels of this incident, another unfortunate turn of events occurred. One of Boyle's laboratory assistants accidentally spilled a bottle of sulfuric acid on the bureau where Boyle kept his papers. The highly corrosive liquid seeped into the drawers and ruined many of Boyle's precious manuscripts. Some of the papers at the bottom of the drawers survived. But many have remnants of the sulfuric acid spill around the edges.

Despite his increasingly failing eyes, much of what Boyle did outside the laboratory during his last years was socialize. Because he had become so renowned in the scientific community and London at large, tons of people stopped by Pall Mall daily to engage him in conversation. The visits got to be so frequent that Boyle devised a visiting schedule. He constructed a board to put on the door of Katherine's home. It listed the days he'd be home. Tuesday and Friday mornings and Wednesday and Saturday afternoons were off limits. Next to the board, he included an announcement, which read:

> **Mr. Boyle finds himself obliged to intimate to those of his friends and acquaintances who are wont to do him the honor of visiting him, [that his] skilful and friendly physician, seconded by his best friends, [have advised him not to see so many people].**

In addition to keeping up with the gossip of the day, Boyle focused on getting his financial affairs and real estate in Ireland in order. He settled up his rents and made sure all his papers were in good standing. Then, he commissioned two portraits. One was painted by a celebrated German artist, Johann Kerseboom. The other was an ivory medallion painted by French artist Jean Cavalier, which was later made into a brass cast by

Robert Boyle

Many later portraits of Robert Boyle were based on the one of him painted by Johann Kerseboom. The German-born Kerseboom moved to London in the 1680s and became a succesful portraitist.

Swedish coin collector Carl Reinhold Berch in 1729. As he had done in the past, Boyle distributed copies of these portraits to friends, family, and colleagues in the scientific community.

Boyle also drew up a last will and testament. In it, he left his property and land in Ireland to his older brother Richard, Earl of Burlington. He made arrangements for all of his scholarly papers to go to Katherine, as well as a ring. He left instructions for her to wear it "in remembrance of a Brother that truely honour'd and most dearly Lov'd her." To the rest of his surviving family members, certain friends, colleagues, and laboratory assistants, he left his tools, clothes, linens, and cash. Robert Hooke was given his most prized microscope. A large portion of his money was designated for charity and religious institutions.

Finally, Boyle published *Experimenta & Observationes Physicae* (*Physical Experiments and Observations*) in 1691. It was a collection of miscellaneous material, mostly dating back to his earlier years in the laboratory. Among other topics, the book's sections included a treatise on magnetism, an additional critique of humorism, and a series of ten reports of strange occurrences in nature. It was the last book Boyle published before he died.

THE DEATH OF A GENIUS

In the autumn of 1691, both Boyle and his sister Katherine became deathly ill. The sickness lasted for months and the two were on bed rest for weeks on end. Unfortunately, neither sibling got better. On December 23, the great Lady Ranelagh died. Three days later, she was buried in the chancel of St. Martin-in-the-Fields church.

The death of his truest lifelong companion shocked and devastated Boyle. He had always assumed that she'd outlive him. Some scholars believe that his sorrow accelerated his own demise. Just four days after Katherine was laid to rest, Boyle took his last breath. He died on December 30.

At his request, Boyle's funeral on January 7, 1692, was basic. Still, more than 100 mourners came to pay their respects to the esteemed scientist, including many members of the Royal Society as well as other mathematicians, astronomers, and philosophers from abroad. Per his instructions, Boyle was buried alongside his sister Katherine in St. Martin-in-the-Fields.

Boyle's death was a somber affair. But what happened to his personal collection of books is an even more unfortunate coda to the story of Boyle's prolific

> Today the Royal Society meets in Carlton House Terrace, in the St. James's section of London, to debate on all matters of science, mathematics, and philosophy.

life. Because of a mix-up in the arrangements, much of his library was sold for far too little money. Some of the books even ended up on the shelves at second-hand bookstores. Others were mixed in with the public's books and sold at auction. Though the Royal Society is

BOYLE

This statue of Robert Boyle at Government Buildings in Dublin, Ireland, is a testament to the scientist's long-lasting legacy.

in possession of most of his more notable works, much of Boyle's personal correspondence was also lost.

But perhaps the saddest development after Boyle's death was the fate of the church that housed his and Katherine's remains. In 1720, it was demolished. No records were kept of the disposal of the dead buried there. The last resting places of Robert and Katherine are still unknown.

BOYLE'S LASTING IMPACT

Robert Boyle was one of the most important thinkers in the Scientific Revolution. His work in developing a law that governed the behavior of gases made possible our understanding of how light and sound travel in a vacuum. Thanks to Boyle, we realize the necessity of paying close attention to failed experiments in addition to successful ones. If it weren't for his discoveries, our grasp of chemistry—that the behavior of substances can be defined by examining the motion of atoms—would be vastly different than it is today.

But though Boyle is best known for advancing the world of science, it is important to remember that he was also a deeply spiritual man who used his pen and his purse to support philanthropic causes. Some scholars criticize him for evangelizing, especially in third-world cultures. But others praise his efforts to have the Bible translated into different languages so it could be read by all.

In his will, Boyle instructed that a series of religious speeches should be periodically delivered in the years after his death. Called the Boyle Lectures, these discourses explored the benefits of living a pious life. They also used the miraculous design of the human body as proof of the existence of an all-knowing God. Finally, they expounded God's wisdom in creating the universe by allowing for the existence of gravity and the movement of bodies throughout time and space. Updated versions of the Boyle Lectures are still delivered at Gresham College to this day.

Combining science and religion, nature and philosophy, Boyle was truly an iconic figure of the Scientific Revolution. He never married, nor did he become a father. But the man had a profound effect on his siblings, neighbors, friends, and colleagues—and on history. His words and writings changed the face of science for future generations. Perhaps the seventeenth-century poet Samuel Boroden encapsulated his legacy best:

Then shone the learned, the industrious Boyle
And sought out Truth with an unweary'd toil;
Boyle on Experiment alone rely'd
And Nature, which he lov'd, was still his guide.

Timeline

1627   Robert Boyle is born on January 25 in County Waterford, Ireland.

1635   Eight-year-old Robert and his older brother Francis leave Ireland to attend Eton College in Windsor, England.

1639   Robert and Francis leave Eton and embark for a multiyear tour of Europe. Their tutor, Isaac Marcombes, educates them along the way.

1643   Patriarch Richard Boyle dies on September 15. He leaves Stalbridge Manor and other lands throughout Ireland and England to Robert.

1644   Boyle returns from the grand tour abroad. He briefly moves in with his sister Katherine.

1646   Boyle's inheritance is settled, and he moves to Stalbridge in Dorset, England. He spends nearly a decade there.

1648   Boyle begins work on *Seraphic Love*, which is not published until 1659.

1649   Boyle sets up his first laboratory and begins conducting experiments at Stalbridge.

1656   Boyle moves to Oxford.
          Boyle begins meeting with members of the Invisible College.

1660   The Royal Society is founded in London, England. *New Experiments Physico-Mechanical, Touching the Spring of Air and Its Effect* is published.

1661 *The Sceptical Chymist* is published—a groundbreaking book that earned him the title "Father of Chemistry."

1662 The second edition of *New Experiments Physico-Mechanical, Touching the Spring of the Air and Its Effects* is published. In the appendix, he describes what later becomes Boyle's law.

1666 Much of London is destroyed in the Great Fire. Boyle publishes his treatise on corpuscularism, *The Origine of Formes and Qualities*.

1668 Boyle moves back in with Katherine in London. A year later, he's elected director of the East India Company.

1670 Boyle suffers a stroke. Still, he publishes a number of influential works over the next decade that unite science and religion, including *Some Considerations about the Reconcileableness of Reason and Religion*.

1684 Boyle demonstrates a new interest in medicine; he publishes *Memoirs for the Natural History of Humane Blood*.

1691 Katherine dies on December 23.
Boyle dies seven days later on December 30.

Glossary

ALCHEMIST A person who believed in the medieval philosophy of turning metals into gold and the discovery of a stone that could prolong life forever.

ALKALINE Having a pH greater than seven; non-acidic.

ASTROPHYSICIST An astronomer who studies the physics of celestial bodies in space.

CAPACIOUS Spacious.

CELIBACY Not having sex.

COMBUSTIBLE Able to catch fire.

COPIOUS Many in number.

CORPUSCULARIANISM The belief that all matter is made up of tiny "corpuscles" or particles.

EVANGELIZING Attempting to convert (usually with regard to religious beliefs).

FRICTION Surface resistance to motion inflicted on an object.

HELIOCENTRIC Relating to the theory that the planets revolve around the Sun; Sun-centric.

HYPOTHESIS A proposed guess or idea in an argument or experiment.

INVERSELY RECIPROCAL A state when an increase in one results in a decrease in another (usually in mathematics or science, with regard to proportions).

OMNISCIENCE Knowing all things.

PALL A dark cloud or mood.

Parliamentarians Supporters of the Parliament, as opposed to the king, during the English Civil Wars.

pH In chemistry, a measure of how acidic or basic a solution is. The range is 0–14, with 7 being neutral and 0 being the most acidic.

Prestigious Fancy; having an elevated status.

Prolific Producing things in large numbers.

Royalists Supporters of the king as the head of state during the English Civil Wars.

Tutelage Instruction; educational teaching.

Velocity Speed; the rate at which an object covers a certain distance.

For More Information

American Association for the Advancement of Science (AAAS)
1200 New York Avenue NW
Washington, DC 20005
(202) 326-6400
Website: http://www.aaas.org
AAAS is the world's largest multidisciplinary scientific society, with members in more than ninety-one countries. Its mission is to advance science, engineering, and innovation throughout the world for the benefit of all people.

Canada Science & Technology Museum
PO Box 9724, Station T
Ottawa, ON K1G 5A3
Canada
(613) 991-3044
Website: http://cstmuseum.techno-science.ca
Recently renovated with brand-new permanent, temporary, and traveling exhibits, this is Canada largest museum dedicated to science and technology.

Chemical Heritage Foundation
315 Chestnut Street
Philadelphia, PA 19106
(215) 925-2222
Website: https://www.chemheritage.org
With a library, museum, and archive center, the CHF is an organization dedicated to telling the stories of the people behind scientific breakthroughs and innovations. The foundation also publishes a magazine called *Distillations*.

The Chemical Institute of Canada
130 Slater Street, Suite 550
Ottawa, ON K1P 6E2
Canada
(613) 232-6252
Website: http://www.cheminst.ca
The Chemical Institute of Canada provides information about available science fairs, scholarships, and the Canadian chemistry contest. Its three constituent societies are the Canadian Society for Chemistry (CSC), the Canadian Society for Chemical Engineering (CSChE), and the Canadian Society for Chemical Technology (CSCT).

For More Information

Exploratorium
Pier 15
San Francisco, CA 94111
(415) 528-4444
Website: http://www.exploratorium.edu
The Exploratorium packs more than six hundred interactive exhibits into six main galleries. The museum also hosts online exhibits featuring informative videos, apps, activities, and links to additional science-oriented websites. Founded in 1969, the museum sees itself as an "ongoing exploration of science, art and human perception."

Museum of Science & Industry
5700 S Lake Shore Drive
Chicago, IL 60637
(773) 684-1414
Website: http://www.msichicago.org
Billing itself as the largest science museum in the Western Hemisphere with 400,000 square feet (37,160 square meters) of space, the Museum of Science and Industry in Chicago houses more than 35,000 artifacts, an Omnimax theater, after-school learning programs, and more.

Youth Science Canada
PO Box 297
Pickering, ON L1V 2R4
Canada
(416) 341-0040
Website: https://www.youthscience.ca
This is Canada's leading national organization dedicated to engaging youth in scientific inquiry and critical thinking.

WEBSITES

Because of the changing nature of Internet links, Rosen Publishing has developed an online list of websites related to the subject of this book. This site is updated regularly. Please use this link to access the list:

http://www.rosenlinks.com/LOSR/boyle

For Further Reading

Bortz, Fred. *Johannes Kepler and the Three Laws of Planetary Motion* (Revolutionary Discoveries of Scientific Pioneers). New York, NY: Rosen Publishing, 2014.

Bortz, Fred. *The Sun-Centered Universe and Nicolaus Copernicus* (Revolutionary Discoveries of Scientific Pioneers). New York, NY: Rosen Publishing, 2014.

Challoner, Jack. *Exploring the Mysteries of Genius and Invention* (The STEM Guide to the Universe). New York, NY: Rosen Publishing, 2017.

Curley, Robert, ed. *Scientists and Inventors of the Renaissance.* New York, NY: Rosen Publishing, 2012.

Fortey, Jacqueline. *Great Scientists* (DK Eyewitness Books). New York, NY: DK, 2007.

Grant, John. *Eureka!: 50 Scientists Who Shaped Human History.* San Francisco, CA: Zest Books, 2016.

Gray, Theodore. *Theodore Gray's Completely Mad Science: Experiments You Can Do at Home but Probably Shouldn't.* New York, NY: Black Dog & Leventhal, 2016.

Heilbron, John L., ed. *The Oxford Companion to the History of Modern Science.* New York, NY: Oxford University Press, 2003.

Losure, Mary. *Isaac the Alchemist: Secrets of Isaac Newton, Reveal'd.* Somerville, MA: Candlewick Press, 2017.

Miller, Ron. *Recentering the Universe: The Radical Theories of Copernicus, Kepler, Galileo, and Newton.* Minneapolis, MN: Twenty-First Century Books, 2013.

Mooney, Carla. *Chemistry: Investigate the Matter That Makes Up Your World* (Inquire and Investigate). White River Junction, VT: Nomad Press, 2016.

Nardo, John. *The Scientific Revolution* (World History Series). Farmington Hills, MI: Lucent Books, 2011.

O'Leary, Denyse. *What Are Newton's Laws of Motion?* (Shaping Modern Science). New York, NY: Crabtree Publishing Company, 2011.

Roscoe, Kelly, and Mick Isle. *Aristotle: The Father of Logic* (The Greatest Greek Philosophers). New York, NY: Rosen Publishing, 2016.

BIBLIOGRAPHY

Boyle, Robert. *The Works of the Honourable Robert Boyle. In Six Volumes.* London, UK: J. and F. Rivington, 1772. https://archive.org/stream/bub_gb_LqYrAQAAMAAJ#page/n13/mode/2up.

Chemical Heritage Foundation. "Robert Boyle." July 15, 2015. https://www.chemheritage.org/historical-profile/robert-boyle.

Famous Scientists. "Robert Boyle." November 2, 2015. http://www.famousscientists.org/robert-boyle.

Hunter, Michael. *Boyle: Between God and Science.* New Haven, CT: Yale University Press, 2009.

Hunter, Michael. "The Life and Thought of Robert Boyle." Birkbeck College, University of London. Retrieved October 17, 2016. http://www.bbk.ac.uk/boyle/biog.html.

Hunter, Michael. "Robert Boyle: An Introduction." Birkbeck College, University of London. Retrieved October 17, 2016. http://www.bbk.ac.uk/Boyle/boyle_learn/boyle_introduction.htm.

Levere, Trevor H. *Transforming Matter: A History of Chemistry from Alchemy to the Buckyball.* Baltimore, MB: JHU Press, 2001.

MacIntosh, J. J., and Peter Anstey. "Robert Boyle." *Stanford Encyclopedia of Philosophy,* August 18, 2014. http://plato.stanford.edu/entries/boyle.

Masson, Flora. *Robert Boyle: A Biography.* London, UK: Constable & Company, Ltd., 1914. https://archive.org/details/robertboylebiogr00massrich.

Newman, William R., and Lawrence M. Principe. *Alchemy Tried in the Fire: Starkey, Boyle, and the Fate of Helmontian Chymistry.* Chicago, IL: University of Chicago Press, 2002.

Newth, John. "Robert Boyle of Stalbridge Park." *Dorset Magazine*, April 2013. http://www.dorsetlife.co.uk/2013/04/robert-boyle-of-stalbridge-park.

O'Connor, J. J., and E. F. Robertson. "Robert Boyle." School of Mathematics and Statistics, University of St. Andrews, Scotland, 2000. http://www-history.mcs.st-and.ac.uk/Biographies/Boyle.html

O'Hare, P. A. "Robert Boyle: Pioneer of Experimental Chemistry." Books at Iowa, 1988. http://ir.uiowa.edu/cgi/viewcontent.cgi?article=1149&context=bai.

The Robert Boyle Summer School. "Robert Boyle." Retrieved October 17, 2016. http://www.robertboyle.ie/about-boyle.

Robinson, Andrew, ed. *The Scientists: An Epic of Discovery.* New York, NY: Thames & Hudson, 2012. pp. 101, 104–109.

The Royal Society. "History." 2016. https://royalsociety.org/about-us/history.

Bibliography

Severance, Diana, Ph.D. "Robert Boyle Converted in a Thunderstorm." Christianity.com, July 2007. http://www.christianity.com/church/church-history/timeline/1601-1700/robert-boyle-converted-in-a-thunderstorm-11630102.html.

Sunshine, Glenn. "Robert Boyle (1627–1691)." *Christian Worldview Journal*, July 9, 2012. http://www.colsoncenter.org/the-center/columns/indepth/18094-robert-boyle-1627-1691.

Westfall, Richard S. "Boyle, Robert." The Galileo Project. Retrieved October 17, 2016. http://galileo.rice.edu/Catalog/NewFiles/boyle.html.

Woodall, David L. "The Relationship Between Science and Scripture in the Thought of Robert Boyle." *Perspectives on Science and Christian Faith*, March 1997. http://www.asa3.org/ASA/PSCF/1997/PSCF3-97Woodall.html.

INDEX

A

air pressure, 50
alchemy, 35, 60, 61
Amorous Controversies, The, 29
Aretology or Ethicall Elements, The, 29
Aristotle, 4, 6, 19, 20, 33, 51, 61–63, 65, 82

B

Bacon, Sir Francis, 32–35, 58, 80
Battle of Drogheda, 37
Battle of Dunbar, 37
Battle of Liscarroll, 23
Battle of Marston Moor, 25
Battle of Preston, 37
Battle of Worcester, 39
Berch, Carl Reinhold, 89
Big Bang, 43
bloodletting, 82–83
Boroden, Samuel, 94
Boyle, Francis (brother), 12, 16, 21
Boyle Lectures, 94
Boyle, Lewis (brother), 21
Boyle, Richard (brother), 89
Boyle, Richard (father), 9, 12, 16, 21, 23, 27
Boyle, Robert
childhood, 9–12
education, 12–36
eyesight, 40, 87
illness, 40, 75, 82, 84
legacy, 80–94
publications, 4, 6, 29, 45, 50, 55, 58, 62, 64, 72, 74, 75, 76, 79, 80, 84, 86, 89
religious beliefs, 17–18, 19–30, 76–79, 93–94
scientific career, 37–79
Boyle's law, 6, 48–51, 67
bubonic plague, 68–70
Burnell, Jocelyn Bell, 44

C

Catholics, 4, 21
Cavlier, Jean, 87
Certain Physiological Essays and Other Tracts, 58, 64
Charles I, 21, 24, 37, 84
Charles II, 37, 43, 69, 70, 73, 74, 84
chemistry, 6, 7, 44, 45, 52, 58–67, 76, 93
cold, 61, 64–66, 70
Collins, Samuel, 66
composition of matter, 61–62
Copernicus, Nicolaus, 4–7, 80

Index

corpuscluarianism, 72
Cromwell, Oliver, 37–39

D
Darwin, Charles, 43
Descartes, René, 42, 72, 80
Dublin Castle, 21

E
East India Company, 76–78
Einstein, Albert, 43
English Civil War, 24, 37, 38
Eton College, 13–14, 16, 26

F
Faithorne, William, 67
Fenton, Lady Catherine (mother), 9

G
Galilei, Galileo, 6, 8, 18–20, 30, 80
Gassendi, Pierre, 42, 72
Glorious Revolution, 84, 85
gravity, 18, 20, 43, 80, 94
Great Fire, 70–72
Great Rebellion. *See* English Civil War
Gresham College, 30, 42, 53–55, 70

Guericke, Otto von, 45

H
Hartlib, Samuel, 30
Hawking, Stephen, 43
heliocentric, 6, 30
humorism, 82, 89
Hodgkin, Dorothy, 44
Hooke, Robert, 45, 46, 48, 69, 70, 75, 80, 89

I
International Alchemy Guild, 61
Invisible College, 30, 32, 40, 42
Irish Rebellion, 21, 22

J
James II, 84
Jones, Arthur, 27

K
Kepler, Johannes, 6
Kerseboom, Johann, 87, 88
Killigrew, Elixabeth, 16

L
laws of motion, 30
laws of planetary motion, 30

Leaning Tower of Pisa, 20
Lismore Castle, 9, 10
Locke, John, 81–82
lost papers, 86

M
Mallet, John, 75
Marcombes, Isaac, 16–18, 21
Masson, Flora, 53
Mercury, 42
Mersenne, Marin, 30
Micrographia, 45
Middle Ages, 4, 60, 61

N
New Experiments Physico-Mechanical, Touching the Spring of Air and Its Effect, 8, 48, 49, 52, 56, 74
New Experiments and Observations Touching Cold, 64, 66
Newton, Isaac, 8, 43, 80

O
Oldenburg, Henry, 55, 75
Origine of Formes and Qualities, The, 64, 72
Oughtred, William, 32

Oxford University, 40, 45

P
Pall Mall, 73, 74, 87
Paracelsus, 58–59, 61–63
Parliamentarians, 21, 24–26
pH indicator, 62
philosopher's stone, 60
Philosophical Transactions, 43
Principia, 80
properties of air, 46

R
Ramakrishnan, Venki, 44
Ranelagh, Lady Katherine (sister), 26–28, 40, 73, 75, 87, 89, 90, 93
Royal Observatory, 42
Royal Charter, 43
Royal Society, 6, 40, 43–44, 52–55, 69–70, 90–91, 93
Royalists, 21, 24–26, 36–37, 39

S
Sceptical Chymist, The, 8, 62–64, 72
scientific method, 32–35, 46, 82

Index

Scientific Revolution, 4, 6, 8, 34–35, 41, 51, 53, 56, 81, 83, 84, 93, 94
Seraphic Love, 29
Some Considerations about the Reconcileableness of Reason and Religion, 64, 76
speech impediment, 11
St. Giles-in-the-Fields, 68
St. Martin-in-the-Fields, 90
St. Paul's Cathedral, 70–71
Stalbridge Manor, 16, 26, 28, 35, 37, 64
Starkey, George, 30, 35

T

temperature, 65–66
Tower of London, 35
Trinity College, 34, 40, 42

V

vacuum, 20, 44–48, 67, 93

W

Wadham College, 40
Ward, Seth, 42
Wilkins, John, 40
Wotton, Sir Henry, 13, 16
Wren, Christopher, 42, 70, 72, 79, 80

ABOUT THE AUTHOR

Alexis Burling is a writer from Portland, Oregon. She spent many years researching fascinating scientific discoveries as a contributor to *SuperScience* and *Math*, two of Scholastic's preeminent in-classroom magazines. She has also published dozens of books for young readers on a variety of topics ranging from current events and career advice to biographies of famous people such as Robert Boyle.

PHOTO CREDITS

Cover, p. 1 (portrait) Stock Montage/Archive Photos/Getty Images; cover, p. 1 (background) Photos.com/Thinkstock; p. 5 InnervisionArt/Shutterstock.com; p. 7 Reproduced by permission of Chatsworth Settlement Trustees/Bridgeman Images; p. 10 walshphotos/Shutterstock.com; pp. 13, 41, 69 Hulton Archive/Getty Images; p. 15 Michael Nicholson/Corbis Historical/Getty Images; pp. 16–17 DEA/G. Dagli Orti/De Agostini/Getty Images; p. 20 Angelo Vianello/Shutterstock.com; pp. 22–23 Universal History Archive/Universal Images Group/Getty Images; p. 25 Photo 12/Universal Images Group/Getty Images; pp. 31, 63, 90–91 Science & Society Picture Library/Getty Images; p. 33 Georgios Kollidas/Shutterstock.com; pp. 38–39, 46, 54–55, 78 Print Collector/Hulton Archive/Getty Images; p. 47 Dorling Kindersley/Thinkstock; p. 49 Universal Images Group/Getty Images; pp. 50–51 Thanapun/Shutterstock.com; pp. 56-57 Photo Researchers, Inc/Alamy Stock Photo; pp. 58–59 Leemage/Corbis Historical/Getty Images; p. 65 rokopix/Shutterstock.com; p. 71 English School/Art Images/Getty Images; pp. 74, 88 DEA Picture Library/De Agostini/Getty Images; p. 81 Heritage Images/Hulton Archive/Getty Images; p. 83 Apic/Hulton Archive/Getty Images; p. 85 Royal Naval College, Greenwich, London, UK/Photo © James Brittain/Bridgeman Images; p. 92 Rob Wilson/Shutterstock.com; back cover, pp. 9, 24, 37, 53, 68, 80 agsandrew/Shutterstock.com; interior pages background Ilya Bolotov/Shutterstock.com

Designer: Brian Garvey; Editor: Amelie von Zumbusch; Photo Researcher: Karen Huang